The Official Ninja Handbook

www.ArnieLightning.com/books

Free Gift

"*It's Okay to Be Different*" is a beautifully illustrated story about accepting and celebrating others for their differences. It's a great way to teach children to appreciate and accept others for who they are.

To claim your FREE GIFT, simply go to www.ArnieLightning.com/freegift and enter your email address. Shortly thereafter, I will send you a free eBook for you to enjoy!

Please visit: www.ArnieLightning.com/freegift

It was late in the night, and Yoshi the kid ninja was having trouble sleeping. He peered through the high windows of the stone walls of the ninja house, studying the starry Japanese sky.

"I'm just a kid," thought Yoshi, "but I want to be the best ninja possible! I'm tired of blending in with all the other kid ninjas. Tomorrow, I'll start on my journey to greatness, and I won't stop until I get there!"

In the morning, Yoshi told the Ninja Master that he wanted to be great.

"You already are great, Yoshi!" said the Ninja Master, who was much kinder than most would have figured.

But Yoshi shook his head. "I want to be special," he said. "I want to set myself apart as a ninja."

"You are serious about this, I can see that," the Ninja Master said after a long pause. "Wait right here."

When he returned, he was carrying a scroll. He handed it to Yoshi. It read, *The Official Ninja Handbook.*

"For me?" gasped Yoshi.

The Ninja Master nodded. "If you take these rules to heart, you will set yourself apart as a ninja in no time," he said.

Yoshi was very excited. He couldn't wait to get started! The first rule in the scroll read, "Stay healthy and active with plenty of exercise."

1. Stay healthy and active with plenty of exercise.

Yoshi's ninja training already provided a lot of exercise, but he figured it couldn't hurt to get more. When he and other kid ninjas swam in the river that morning, Yoshi swam twice as far as everyone else! And when they practiced scaling walls, Yoshi climbed twice as high!

Yoshi made it a habit to go above and beyond what was expected of him.

Everyone was impressed with Yoshi's energy. He continued day after day, but soon it was time to add the second rule to his daily routine.

It said, "Keep your clothing clean, pressed, and spotless, washing it if streaks appear."

2. Keep your clothing clean, pressed, and spotless, washing it if streaks appear."

Since ninjas are so active, Yoshi had to do a lot of extra laundry to follow this rule. He soon found that it was worth it, because all of his friends were commenting on how professional he looked!

Rule number three said, "Keep your sword shiny at all times!" That was easier said than done after dueling practice, but Yoshi polished his faithful weapon as often as necessary.

"Look at Yoshi's shiny sword!" the other kid ninjas gasped.

The next rule in the handbook was something that was very important to a ninja, but which Yoshi had always struggled with. It said, "When sneaking around be light, quiet, and speedy."

Yoshi knew it was important for ninjas to make very little noise. So he spent hours of his spare time practicing until he was able to sneak up on his friends without getting caught!

"I'm living by four of these rules every single day!" Yoshi thought proudly. "But I can't stop there!"

Rule number five said, "Eat a balanced diet, eat your vegetables, and avoid too many sweets."

That was a hard rule to follow because Yoshi loved dessert! He found that when he filled up on sushi, fish, fruits, vegetables, and other nutritious foods, he only had enough room left for a very small dessert.

The next rule told Yoshi, "The sum of the team equals far more than the sum of the individuals."

Yoshi played ball games with his friends and practiced utilizing the strengths of teammates to get the best out of each player. He quickly learned that a strong team is much more powerful than an individual player. He also learned that by doing his best it also made the team better.

The next rule read, "Treat others as you would expect to be treated."

When Yoshi read that rule, he knew he was up for the challenge. So he planned a surprise party for the Ninja Master's birthday! He planned a huge celebration and invited all the kid ninjas.

Rule number eight confused Yoshi.

"Know when to fight and when to walk away."

He asked the Ninja Master about it. The older and wiser ninja told Yoshi, "Some things are worth fighting for, like when you're in danger or when you know something is terribly wrong and you have no other choice. But most of the time, you can settle things peacefully with others through communication. Fight only for what you believe in."

Later that day, Yoshi saw one of his ninja friends being bullied. Yoshi decided to stand up for his friend and defend him. Yoshi remembered the wise words from the Ninja Master and resolved the dispute through communication.

The next rule read, "Be honest, fair, and kind. Use your strengths (physically, mentally, and emotionally) to help and bring out the best in others."

That day, Yoshi was extra-kind to the villagers when he went to the fish market with some of the adult ninjas. He gave some coins to a child who couldn't afford a fish and he helped an elderly woman cross the road!

The last rule in *The Official Ninja Handbook* read, "Above all, have confidence in yourself. Believe that you are special simply because you are you. Instead of feeling bad about yourself or wishing you were someone else, celebrate who you are. The very best ninjas are happy being themselves! You should always strive to be the best YOU!"

10 . Above all, have confidence in yourself. Believe that you are special simply because you are you. Instead of feeling bad about yourself or wishing you were someone else, celebrate who you are. The very best ninjas are happy being themselves!
You should always strive to be the best YOU!

Yoshi remembered that rule whenever he felt down or discouraged. He knew that no matter what happened, he always had control over his reactions. He chose to put his best foot forward and do his best in any given situation.

Soon, the Ninja Master recognized Yoshi's confidence and praised him for it. "I see that you are comfortable with who you are, Yoshi," smiled the Ninja Master. "You are well on your way to becoming a very great ninja, indeed!"

If Yoshi can be a great ninja, there's no reason you can't do the same. Just follow the rules in *The Official Ninja Handbook*, be your best self, and have fun doing it!

My Ninja Rules

How will you use the rules in *The Official Ninja Handbook* to be your best self?
Be like Yoshi. Create a plan for yourself below and take action!

_____

_____

_____

_____

_____

_____

_____

_____

_____

_____

_____

_____

About the Author

Arnie Lightning is a dreamer. He believes that everyone should dream big and not be afraid to take chances to make their dreams come true. Arnie enjoys writing, reading, doodling, and traveling. In his free time, he likes to play video games and run. Arnie lives in Mississippi where he graduated from The University of Southern Mississippi in Hattiesburg, MS.

For more books by Arnie Lightning please visit:
www.ArnieLightning.com/books